George was an ordinary dollar bill who lived in the leather wallet of a school janitor named Mr. Juan Carlos.

He didn't like being alone.

# TWO DOLLAR$, ONE WALLET

## ONE WALLET

WRITTEN AND
ILLUSTRATED BY A
GROUP OF THIRD
GRADE STUDENTS
AT MCKINLEY
ELEMENTARY IN
BURBANK,
CALIFORNIA

Scholastic Inc.    New York  Toronto  London  Auckland  Sydney  Mexico City  New Delhi  Hong Kong  Buenos Aires

ORIGINAL COVER

This book is dedicated to:

Our teacher Mrs. Angie D'Mello

Our Moms & Dads

And "Superman"

He tried to talk to a photo I.D., but the I.D. was too shy.

"Who turned on the lights?" said George as
Mr. Juan Carlos opened the wallet.
George felt something cold and hard touch his fluffy hair.
It was a coin!

"Please don't wake my baby,
I just got him to sleep!" yelped a soft voice.

"Sorry," said George, blushing.
The Sacagawea coin was shiny, gold, and beautiful.

George felt smelly and wrinkled compared to Sacagawea.
"I'm sorry I yelled at you. You look beat up and crumpled," said Sacagawea, "But you look familiar."

"I was the first president!" said George.

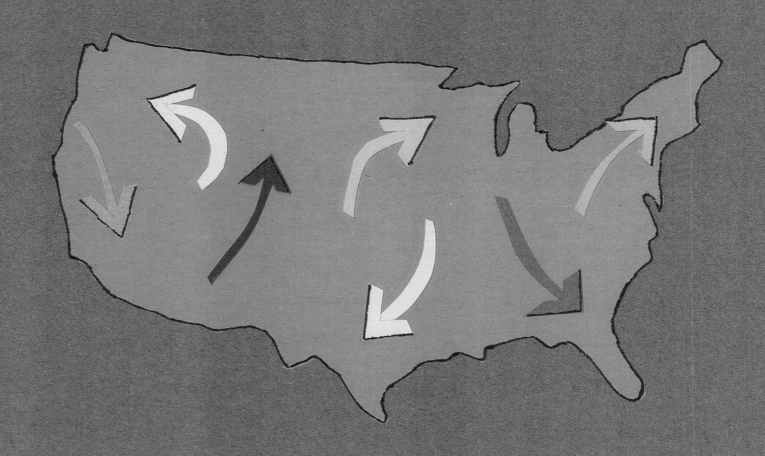

"But I've been around the country a lot.
It's kind of a funny story."
"I love funny stories," said Sacagawea.

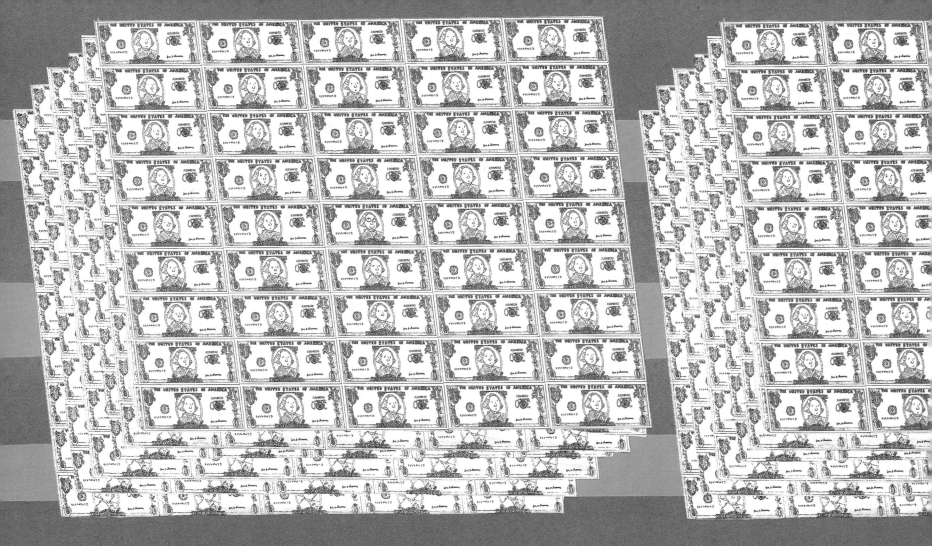

"I was born in Washington, D.C. at the United States
Bureau of Engraving and Printing.  A huge machine printed me,"
replied George.  "I was put in a bag on a bed of my brothers.

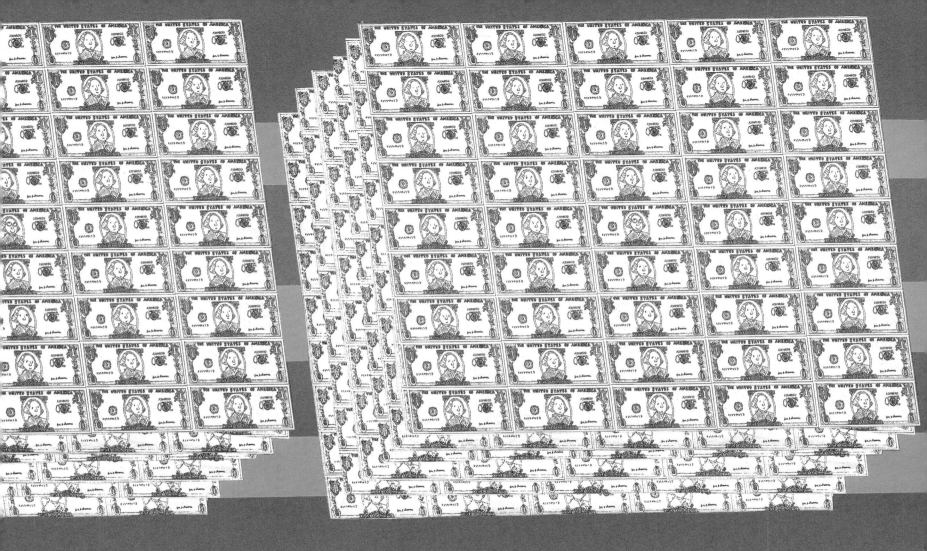

The next thing I knew, I was at a bank!"

"A little girl got me
out of the bank.
She traded me for a
chocolate sprinkled donut."

"The donut maker spent me on a dance game at the arcade," said George.

"Then the arcade cashier took me to a dog bakery, where I got wet and … slobbery."

"Being slid into the claw machine at the toy store hurt, but I won a huge pink bunny!"

"Next, I was used to buy some underwear at a dollar store. It was rather embarrassing." Sacagawea giggled.

"I visited the zoo where I saw a penny get squished flat.

I hope Mr. Lincoln is okay." said George.

"After that, I was used to buy a raffle ticket at a school carnival."

Raffle Ticket
Number
1316236AZ19NRJG
ONE

"I was given as change when someone bought a hot dog. You see this?" George looked at a stain on his shoulder. "Mustard!"

"I survived the washing machine, although it made me dizzy."

"So hanging in the sun felt like a vacation," said George.

"Then Mr. Juan Carlos put me into his wallet," said George.
"Wow! That's an amazing story," said Sacagawea.

"It's very nice to meet you." She smiled at him.

"I'm famous because I helped the explorers Lewis and Clark find their way to the Pacific Ocean" said Sacagawea. "My story is shorter than yours. The tooth fairy traded me for a tooth. A nice little girl named Violet put me in her pocket, but there was a hole and I fell out."

"I stayed on the cold playground until Mr. Juan Carlos
picked me up," said Sacagawea, "And here I am!"
"I cannot tell a lie," said George.
"It's nice to finally meet a friend!"

Suddenly –

– the wallet opened and George felt a tug.
He was being taken out of the wallet!
"Nooooo!" yelled George.
"Goodbye, George!" said Sacagawea.
But she felt herself move, too.

Mr. Juan Carlos put them in Violet's hand.

She smiled at Sacagawea and George. And they both wondered...

...where their adventures would take them next.

# MEET THE AUTHORS

Clockwise (from left): John Alijijian, Noel Pennington, Russell Uvas, Julia Guglielmo, Marion Hunter, Sara Cohen, Henry Keeney

Kids Are Authors®

Books written by children for children

The Kids Are Authors® Competition was established in 1986 to encourage children to read and to become involved
in the creative process of writing.

Since then, thousands of children have written and illustrated books as participants in the Kids Are Authors® Competition.

The winning books in the annual competition are published by Scholastic Inc.
and are distributed by Scholastic Book Fairs throughout the United States.

For more information:

Kids Are Authors® 1080 Greenwood Blvd.; Lake Mary, FL 32746 or visit our web site at: www.scholastic.com/kidsareauthors

ISBN 13: 978-0-545-51581-8          12 11 10 9 8 7 6 5 4 3 2 1

Cover design by Bill Henderson

Audiobook production by Ear Candy Sound

Sound Engineer: Maui Holcomb          Producer: Pamela Holcomb

Printed and bound in the U.S.A.          First Printing, July 2012